W9-CHI-792

For Mom, who took
us on the journey.

For Jonathan.

FAMILIUS

Published by Familius LLC, www.familius.com

Familius books are available at special discounts for bulk purchases for sales promotions or for
family or corporate use. Special editions, including personalized covers, excerpts of existing books,
or books with corporate logos, can be created in large quantities for special needs. For more
information, contact Premium Sales at 559-876-2170 or email specialmarkets@familius.com.

Library of Congress Catalog-in-Publication Data

2014956436

ISBN 978-1-939629-65-4

Cover and book design by David Miles

10 9 8 7 6 5 4 3 2 1

First Edition

book

ILLUSTRATIONS BY

DAVID MILES   NATALIE HOOPES

This is a book.

Black words. On white paper.

No buttons.
No bonus levels.
Not a single sound, in fact.

It's the most quiet, ordinary
thing that could be,
until you learn to look closer,

and closer,

and clos

. . . and you're suddenly in a place
that only you can imagine.

of the sky

butterflies

puddles

your mind,

When you Use

buzzing

x chatons jume
en envoie trois
dépose au pi
s demande de me
re cours à ma t
ien m'habitu
oyaume d
vo

like the su
all of them m
far away that it ma
great distances in sp

stars
are smaller
farther away
kes one's head spi

here imagination scrapes the skies of opportunity,

the forests of what-could-be stretch beyond the horizon,

and the friends of fact and fiction make believe all night long under the milky stars of possibility.

It's your home when
you want to learn.

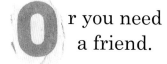 r you need
a friend.

Or you just want to be alone on the highest
mountain on the farthest planet in the universe.

There, no alarm will disturb and no screen will crack.

Because it doesn't have one.
Or an off switch.
Or a password to keep you out.

It will never be sick, because viruses can't catch it.

It will never go dark, because it doesn't need batteries.

Which is fortunate, because in your search for truth,

only light can show you what was imprisoned for so long . . .

. . . and set it free!

Free to fly, free to find, free to embrace for your very own.

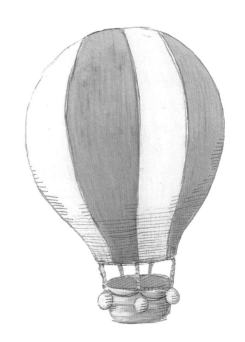

And when your time comes
to a close and the other world
begins to call, don't worry.

You can say goodbye
without feeling sad, because
you know you can come back
as often as you wish.

It will all be here—always close, always near—
because you're the one holding . . .

a book.